Nicholas Breton

No whippinge Nor Trippinge - But a Kinde Friendly

Snippinge.

London, 1601. A Poetical Reply, Moral, Satirical, and Proverbial, During the

Literary Quarrel Between Ben Jonson, John Marston, W. Ingram, of

Cambridge, and others.

Nicholas Breton

No whippinge Nor Trippinge - But a Kinde Friendly Snippinge.
London, 1601. A Poetical Reply, Moral, Satirical, and Proverbial, During the Literary Quarrel Between Ben Jonson, John Marston, W. Ingram, of Cambridge, and others.

ISBN/EAN: 9783337142537

Printed in Europe, USA, Canada, Australia, Japan

Cover: Foto ©Andreas Hilbeck / pixelio.de

More available books at **www.hansebooks.com**

THE ISHAM REPRINTS.

No. 3.

NO WHIPPINGE, NOR TRIP-PINGE : BUT A KINDE FRIENDLY SNIPPINGE.

BY NICHOLAS BRETON.

1601.

No Whippinge, nor Trippinge: but a kinde friendly Snippinge.

LONDON, 1601.

A POETICAL REPLY, MORAL, SATIRICAL, AND PRO-
VERBIAL, DURING THE LITERARY QUARREL BETWEEN
BEN JONSON, JOHN MARSTON, W. INGRAM, OF
CAMBRIDGE, AND OTHERS.

By NICHOLAS BRETON,

AUTHOR OF "THE PILGRIMAGE TO PARADISE," "RAVISHT SOULE
& BLESSED WEEPER," "FLOORISH UPON FANCIE," ETC.

❧

REPRINTED FROM THE ORIGINAL EDITION, LATELY
IN THE POSSESSION OF SIR CHARLES E. ISHAM, BART.,
AND NOW IN THE BRITISH MUSEUM, WITH
A BIBLIOGRAPHICAL PREFACE,

By CHARLES EDMONDS,

EDITOR OF THE "ISHAM SHAKESPEARE OF 1599;" HAKE'S
"NEWES OUT OF POWLES CHURCHYARDE, 1579;" "THE
POETRY OF THE ANTI-JACOBIN," BY CANNING,
HOOKHAM FRERE, G. ELLIS, W.
GIFFORD, ETC.

PUBLISHED BY
ELKIN MATHEWS,
VIGO STREET, LONDON,
MDCCCXCV.

CHISWICK PRESS:—CHARLES WHITTINGHAM AND CO.
TOOKS COURT, CHANCERY LANE, LONDON.

A BIBLIOGRAPHICAL NOTE BY THE DISCOVERER, WHO IS ALSO THE EDITOR.

THAT "Good Wine needs no Bufh" is a good old Englifh proverb, and one that the good old Englifh writer who is now under notice would have heartily endorfed, for no one more frequently ufed proverbs nor more often inculcated their ftudy, as may be feen in the prefent Tractate, and in another production of his publifhed in the fame year. On his great literary abilities, both in profe and verfe, and his power to bound "from grave to gay, from lively to fevere"—it is unneceffary to dilate, for they have been acknowledged by competent authorities from the time when he firft appeared as an author in 1577, till his laft dated work in 1637. Indeed, he was never more appreciated than at the prefent time, as

is evidenced by the jubilant chorus of Biblio-
philes and Bibliographers over the acquiſition
of ſome of the moſt important of his as well
as of other precious books, from the Lamport
Hall Library, by the Britiſh Muſeum authorities, and proudly exhibited by them in the
King's Library there.[1]

This poetical piece by NICHOLAS BRETON,
a Staffordſhire man, was found by the writer of
the preſent notice, together with many other
moſt valuable poetical works of the Elizabe-
than-Jacobean age, in a diſuſed lumber-room
at Lamport Hall, Northamptonſhire, the ſeat
of Sir Charles E. Iſham, Bart., the 23rd Sept.,
1867. What made this literary treaſure-trove
more noteworthy and valuable was, that not
only moſt of the books were in as *clean and
perfeƈt* a ſtate as when iſſued by the printer,
but that many of them—including ſome by

---

[1] "Elizabethan Literature at the Britiſh Muſeum"
is the heading of a highly congratulatory notice on
the poſſeſſion of theſe works, in "The Times" of
Aug. 31, and in "Notes and Queries" of Sept. 15,
1894.

Breton—had never even been *cut open.* THE
GREAT GLORY OF THE ISHAM LIBRARY was
the volume containing the *hitherto unknown
edition* of SHAKESPEARE'S [fo *originally* fpelled]
earlieſt poem, "Venus and Adonis," dated
1599, and the remarkable collection of pieces
entitled the "Paffionate Pilgrime"—thefe laſt
all fathered upon Shakefpeare without his
authority—with pieces by (*Sir*) John Davies
and Marlowe. This volume was in equally
fine prefervation, and in the original vellum
binding, with ſtrings.

The work now under notice was the laſt of
an anonymous Trilogy; arifing out of an attack
upon BEN JONSON by a clique of envious and
rancorous poets and actors, among whom were
MARSTON and DEKKER, for his dictatorial
and generally fcornful manner towards them.
The firſt of the feries was entitled "The
Whipping of the Satyre," by I. W. The
author is conjectured by the late Dr. Brinſley
Nicholfon, who beſtowed much labour on
the matter, to have been WM. INGRAM, of
Cambridge. The fecond, called "The Whip-

per of the Satyre, his Pennance in a White
Sheete, etc.," who is alfo mercilefly attacked,
is undoubtedly John Marfton; while the third
fhows the hand of Breton in every page.

BRETON's work is efpecially valuable. Not
only does he act as a true peacemaker, but ex-
hibits his good qualities in various directions.
His found practical fenfe is fhown throughout
by the ufe he makes of Englifh Proverbs; and
his fcathing rebukes of each clafs of contem-
porary delinquents, and his object-leffons from
human beings, quadrupeds, birds, fifhes, and
fpiders, are remarkably happy. BUT HIS
ALLUSIONS TO HIMSELF, HIS EDUCATION, HIS
LIKES AND DISLIKES, ETC., HAVE ALL THE
CHARM OF A CANDID AUTOBIOGRAPHY.

C. E.

No whippe.

Be loyall, fayes the Lyon, for your life;
Be firme and conftant, fayes the Elephant:
The Doue bids you be louing to your wife:
Be carefull, fayes the Partridge: painefull, the Ant:
Take heede, fayes Rainarde, of the Sycophant:
　Be wakefull, fayes the Cocke: Witty, the Conny:
　And fayes the Dog; looke well vnto your monie.

Haue all the weeke a penne behinde your eare,
And weare your fword on Sundayes, tis enough:
Be not too venturous, nor too full of feare:
Nor ftand too much vpon a double ruffe;
For feare a falling band giue you the cuffe.
Know well your horfe before you fall to ride:
And bid God bleffe the Bride-groom & his Bride.
　　　　　　　　　　　　　　　　Be

No whippe.

Be neither proude, nor enuious, nor vnchaſte;
Leaſt al too late,repentance ouer-take you:(waſte,
And take good heede howe you your wealth doe
Leaſt fooles doe ſcoffe you, & your friends forſake
And thẽ the begger by the ſhulders ſhake you. (you
   Giue vnto all that aske;not askers,all :
   And take heed how you clime,for fear you fall.

Doe well,be true, backe-bite no man,be iuſt;
The Ducke,the Drake,theOwle,do teach you ſo:
Speake what you thinke ; but no more then you
Leaſt vnawares you make your friend your fo(muſt
Be warie, ſayes the Crane; bee wiſe, the Crowe:
   Be gentle,humble,courteous,meeke, & milde,
   And you ſhall be your mothers bleſſed childe.
B 4   Be

No whippe

Be not a churle, nor yet exceed in cheere.
Holdfaſt thine owne, pay truely what thou oweſt:
Sell not too cheape, and doe not buy to deare :
Tell but to few, what ſecret ere thou knoweſt, (eſt:
And take good heed to whom, & what thou ſhew-
    Loue God, thy ſelf, thy wife, thy childrē, friend,
    Neighbour, and ſeruant, and ſo make an end.

Beleeue no newes, till they be nine dayes old,
Nor thẽ too much, although the print approue thẽ:
Miſtake not droſſe for perfeƈt Indian gold; (them:
Nor make friends gods; but as you finde them, loue
And as you know them, keepe thẽ, or remooue thẽ.
    Beware of beauty, and affeƈt no ſlutte :
    And ware the worme before ye cracke the nut
                                                    Be

No whippe.

Learne Englifh Prouerbs, haue them wel by heart,
And count them often on your fingers ends :
Doe not your fecrets to the world impart:
Beware your foes, doe not abufe your friends :
Take heed of flatterers as of hellifh fiends:
　Eate vp your meat, & make cleane all your plat-
　Andmeddle not with any princes matters. (ters,

Reade what is written on the painted cloth;
Doe no man wrong, be good vnto the poore :
Beware the Moufe, the Maggot, and the Moth;
And euer haue an eye vnto the doore :
Truft not a foole, a villaine, nor a whore.
　Goe neat, not gaie; and fpend but as you fpare :
　Andturne the Colte to pafture with the Mare.

Be

No whippe.

Know you a Swaggerer? let him walke along :
Trouble him not in either word,or deed.
He is not borne to put vp open wrong :
Where euery man may of his humour read.
Be filent then good Poet and take heede
  (What euer faults you in his folly fee)
  You doe not talke of fuch a man as he.

If that a great one haue a great defect,
Let not your thought once touch at fuch a thing.
Vnto Superious euer haue refpect :
A Begger muft not looke vpon a King.
Take heede,I fay, is a moft bleffed thing :
  Leaft if you run to farre in fuch a fit,
  A foole may happe to hang for lacke of wit.

Learne

No whippe.

Know you a Gamefter? let him play his game:
But feeke not you to cheat him of his coyne.
Nor to the world doe idly tell his name,
Whofe heedleffe fancie doeth with folly ioyne,
That cannot fee who doeth his wealth purloine:
    Leaft when you name the chance that loft his
    He light on you,& make your noddle ake. (ftake

Know you a Plotter? ftuddy not his Plots,
But leaue the bufie, to their bufineffe:
Leaft while you winde your wits into fuch knots,
You doe too late repent your foolifhneffe,
And while you write of fuch vngodlineffe,
    Finde ere the lines of halfe your rules be red,
    To write of knaues doth bring a foole to bed.

No whippe.

Knowe you a Mifer? let him be fo ftill,
And let his fpirites with his metall melt:
Let him alone to die in his owne ill,
And feede not you on that which he hath felt:
Be not you girded in fo vile a belt:
   Rather praie for him, then fo raile vpon him,
   That all the world may lay their curfes on him.

Knowe you a Spendthrift fecreatly aduife him,
But tell not all the worlde of his expence:
For if fuch kinde of warning you deuife him,
Your courfe maie happe to fall on fuch offence,
As may be put off with an ill defence:
   For many a man that hath his wits afquint,
   Would frowne to fee his folly put in print.
                        Knowe

No whippe.

Know you a drunkeard? loath his drunkennesse:
But doe not laie it open to his foes:
Least in describing his vngodlinesse,
You take your selfe too soundly by the nose:
Who hurts himselfe doth giue vnkindely blowes:
Winke at each faulte & wish it were amended,
And thinke it well that's with repentance ended.

Knowe you a wencher, let his wenche alone,
Winke at his fault, & age will make him leaue it:
And though he doe not, tell not Iohn of Ioane,
For feare that ether you may misconceaue it,
Or tone be hurt when tother doth perceiue it:
   Or while you seeke to make their folly knowne,
   It be a meane to lay abroad your owne.
            B   Knowe

No whippe.

Know you a villaine? let him finde his matche:
And show not you a Matche a villaines skill:
A foolish dogge at euery Curre doeth snatch,
Wordes haue no grace in eloquence of ill:
There is no wrestling with a wicked will:
   Let passe the villaine with his villany,
   Make thou thy match with better company.

Haue you acquaintance with some wicked quean,
Giue her good words, and do not blaze her faults:
Looke in thy soule if it be not vncleane:
And knowe that Sathan all the world assaultes:
Iacob himselfe before the Aungell haultes:
   Sighe for her sinne, but doe not call her whore:
   But learne of Christ, to bid her sinne no more.
                         Knowe

No whippe.

Know'ſt thou a foole? then let him leaue his folly,
Or be ſo ſtil, and with his humour paſſe.
What hath thy wit to do with trolly lolly?
Muſt euery wiſe man ride vpon an Aſſe?
Take heede thou mak'ſt not him a looking glaſſe,
  Wherein the world may too apparant ſee,
  By blazing him, to finde the foole in thee.

Haſt thou eſpied a knaue? care not to know him,
Leſt that thy knowledge get thee little good.
Or if you know him, doe not ſeeke to ſhow him:
Leſt that your head be fear'd to fit his hoode.
Such ſenſe were better neuer vnderſtoode.
  Better to ſee a knaue, and not to ſee,
  Then to be thought a knaue, as well as hee.
                     Knowe

No whippe.

As for thofe fanfies,fictions,or fuch fables,
That fhow in loffe of time abufe of wit:
That neuer look't into thofe holy Tables,
Where doeth the grace of reafons glory fit:
And wifedome findes what is for vertue fit,
  What ere they figure in their dark conftructions,
  They doe but little good in their inftructions.

No,poets,no: I write to yee in loue,
Let not the world haue caufe to laugh at vs:
Let vs our mindes from fuch ill meanes remoue,
As makes good fpirits for to fall out thus:
Let vs our caufes with more care difcuffe: (chide:
  Not bite,nor claw,nor fcoffe, nor check,nor
  But eche mend one, and ware the fall of pride.
                              Know'ft

No whippe.

For let him bragge, and braue it as he lift,
The Poets is a poore profeſſion:
And often times doeth fall on had I wift, (feſſion:
When conſcience makes of inwarde crimes con-
And ſorrow makes the ſpirites interceſſion,
   For mercies pardon, to that time miſſpent,
   Which was the ſoule for better ſeruice lent.

Yet will I ſay that ſome, oh all too fewe,
Doe bend their humors to diuine deſires:
Thoſe I confeſſe, doe in their verſes ſhew,
What vertue, Grace into thoſe ſoules inſpires,
That are inflamed with the heauenly fires:
   Such a good Poet, good if any bee,
   Onely in God, would God that I were hee.

As

No whippe.

Some one will ſay, you are too buſie pated,
An other ſaies the foole is idle headed:
An other ſaies ſuch rakehells would be rated:
An other, ſee, how will to wit is wedded:
An other, ſure the man is poorely ſtedded:
  Hee writ for coine, he knew, nor car'd not what:
  But yet take heede, we muſt not like of that.

Meane while perhaps he ſits within his Cell,
And ſighes to heare how many deſcant on him:
And for a litle muſt his labour ſell,
While ſuch as haue the pence, do preie vpon him:
And he poore ſoule, in want thus wo begon him,
  Curſeth the time, that euer he was borne,
  To vſe his will to make his wit a ſcorne.

No whippe.

Good writers then, if any ſuch yee be,
In verſe or proſe, take well that I doe write:
I wiſh yee all what ere yee heare or ſee ,
Haſte not your wits to bring it vnto light:
Leſt ere you weet you doe repent your ſpight.
    Your friendes ill courſes neuer doe diſcloſe,
    And make your pens no ſwords to hurt yonr foes.

Spend not your thoughts in ſpilling of your wits:
Nor ſpoile your eies, in ſpying of offences.
For howſoeuer you excuſe your fittes,
They carry ſhreud ſuſpect of ill pretences:
And when you ſeeke to make your beſt defences,
    How euer priuate friends will poorly purſe ye,
    If one doe bleſſe yee, fiue to one will curſe ye.
                        Some

No whippe.

The Preachers charge is but to chide for finne,
While Poets fteppes are fhort of fuch a ftate:
And who an others office enters in,
May hope of loue, but fhalbe fure of hate.
T is not a time offences to relate.
   Contentions fooner will begin then end :
   And one may fooner lofe, then keepe a friend.

And he that writes, vnwary of his wordes,
May haue an ill conftruction of the fenfe.
For fortune euer not the right affordes,
Where will doeth gouerne ouer patience,
Who doeth not finde it by experience,
   That points and letters often times mifread,
   Endaunger oft the harmeleffe writers head?
                          Good

No whippe.

For they whofe eyes into the world doe looke,
And canuaffe euery crotchet of conceite,
Whofe wary wittes can hardly be miftooke,
Who neuer feede their fancies with deceite,
Finde this the fruict of euery idle fleight:
    To fhew how enuy doeth her venom fpit,
    Or lacke of wealth doeth fell a little wit.

And while they tumble in their tubbes of coine,
Laugh at their wittes that runne fo far awry :
In learning how to giue the foole the foine,
Miftake the warde & wound them felues thereby:
While only wealth doth laugh at beggery.
    For rowling ftones will neuer gather moffe,
    And raunging wittes doe often liue by loffe.
                       The

No whippe.

Now comes another with a new founde vaine:
And onely falls to reprehenſions:
Who in a kind of ſcoffing chiding ſtraine,
Bringes out I knowe not what in his inuentions:
But I will gheſſe the beſt of his intencions:
 Hee would that all were well, and ſo would I:
 Fooles ſhuld not too much ſhew their foolery,

And would to God it had ben ſo in deed,
The Satyres teeth had neuer bitten ſo:
The Epigrammiſt had not had a ſeede
Of wicked weedes, among his herbes to ſowe,
Nor one mans humor did not others ſhowe,
 Nor Madcap had not ſhowen his madneſſ ſuch,
 And that the whipper had not ierkt ſo much.
          For

No whippe.

(daies:

IS ſtrange to ſee the humors of theſe
How firſt the Satyre bites at imperfectiõs:
The Epigrammiſt in his quips diſplaies
A wicked courſe in ſhadowes of corrections:
The Humoriſt hee ſtrictly makes collections
  Of loth’d behauiours both in youthe and age:
  And makes them plaie their parts vpon a ſtage.

An other Madcappe in a merry fit,
For lacke of witte did caſt his cappe at ſinne:
And for his labour was well tould of it,
For too much playing on that merry pinne:
For that all fiſhes are not of one finne:
  And they that are of cholerick complections,
  Loue not too plain to reade their imperfection
                    Now

to the Reader.

better to my euill fortune. Well, in earneſt, I will entreat all good ſchollers to beare with my lacke of learning, and wiſe men with my lacke of witte, and my creditors with my lacke of mony. Which, though it haue nothing to doe in this Treatiſe, yet entreaty ſometime doeth well with honeſt mindes: which I wiſh, and hope of in them, yea, and all the world that I ſhall haue to doe withall. Leauing therefore the patient to their Paradice, and the diſpleaſed to their better patience, in my loue to all ſchollers (but chiefly to thoſe, that in the ioy of their ſtudies, make vertue their heauen) I Reſt

Your friend, as I finde cauſe.

The Epiftle

ftraungely inueigh againft another, that many shallow wits ftoode and laught at their follies. Now, findinge their labours so toucht with ill tearms, as befitted not the learned to lay open; I thought good, hauing little to doe, to write vnto all such writers, as take pleasure to see their wits plaie with the world, that they will henceforth, before they fall to worke, haue in minde this good prouerbe : Play with mee; but hurt me not : and ieft with me; but difgrace me not; *Leaft that the world this ieft do kindly smother, Why should one foole be angry with an other? Now for my selfe, I protefte that humor of Charitie, that I wish to finde at all their handes that see and will reprooue my folly: for I am none of the seauen wise men, and for the eight, I knowe not where to seeke him. Beare with me then, if out of the principles of a painted cloth I haue pickt out matter to mooue impatience. And if there be any thing out of that poore library, that may take place in any of your good likings, I will honour your good spirits for your kinde acceptations. But, in any wise, what ere you think, giue me no word of comendation: leaft, too glad of such a mischaunce, I truft the*

better

¶ TO ALL GRATIOVS,
Vertuous, Courteous, Honeſt,
Learned,and gentle ſpirits,that are
truely poeticall, & not too fantaſticall:
that will patiently read,indifferently cen-
ſure, and honeſtly ſpeake of the labours
of thoſe wits that meane nothing
but well,the writer hereof wiſh-
eth all contentment, that
a good conditiõ may
deſire.

Y good friendes, if ſuch yee be;
if not, God bleſſe me from yee :
for the world is ſo full of wicked-
neſſe, that a man can meete with
little goodneſſe : Maye it pleaſe
you to vnderſtand,that it was my happe of late,
paſſing through Paules Church yarde, to looke
vpon certaine pieces of Poetrye, where I found
(that it greeues me to ſpeake of)one writer ſo

ſtrangely

NO

VVhippinge, nor

trippinge: but a

kinde friendly

Snippinge.

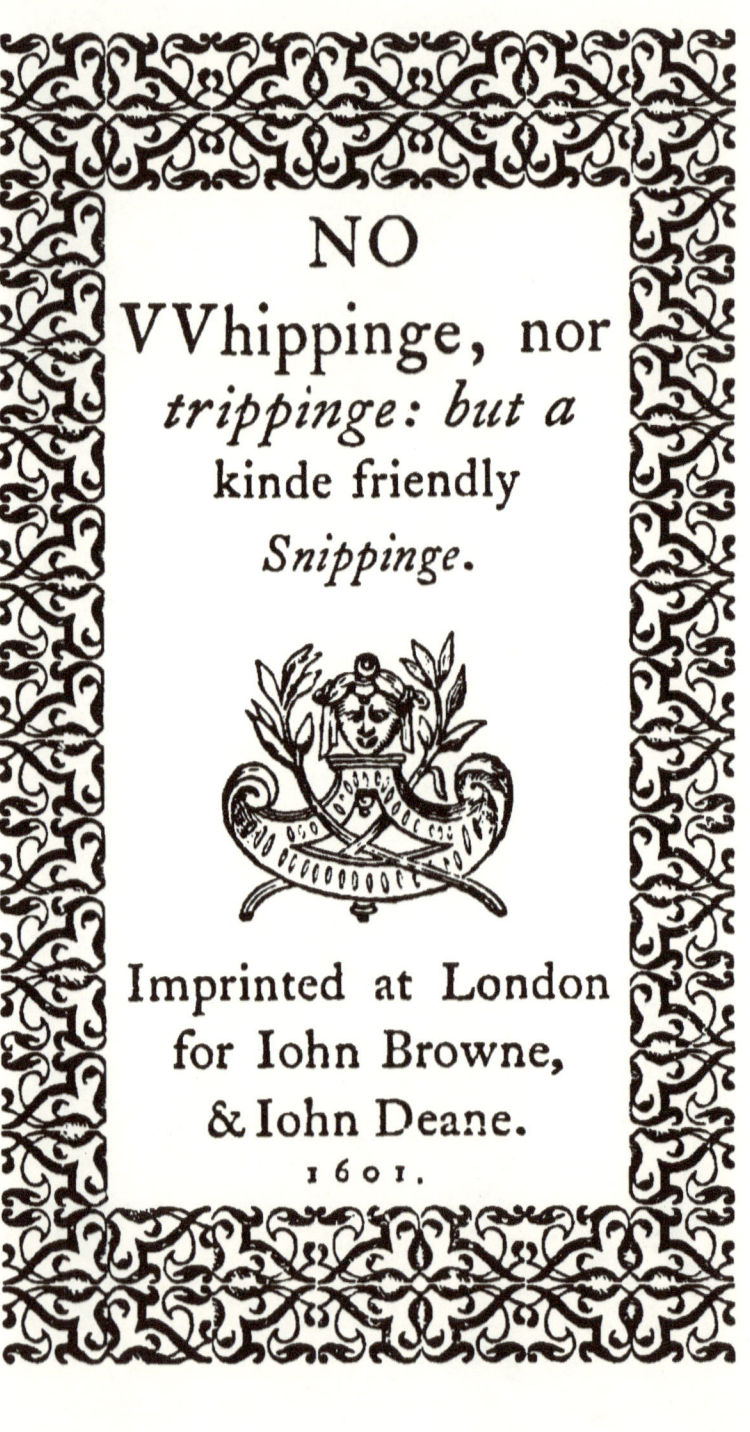

Imprinted at London
for Iohn Browne,
& Iohn Deane.
1601.

No whippe.

Be merry, fayes the Cuckow: lufty, the Frog:
Nimble, the Snaile: the Mag-pye, prouident:
Be thrifty, fayes the Buzzard: cleanly the Hogge:
Honeft, the Bull: the Pigeon refident:
The Popingeare doth bid you to be filent:
    Be valiant, fayes the Horfe: fimple, the Affe;
    A better Dictionary neuer was.

Be gracious, fayes the Kite: gentle, the wafpe:
Be liberall, the Moile: fober, the Hare:
Swift, fayes the Tortoife: vertuous, the Ape:
Pittifull, the Woolfe: mannerly, the Mare:
Thankefull the Eagle: bountifull, the Stare:
    Trufty, the Iack-daw: faithfull, fayes the Hearne:
    What better leffons then the Birdes doe learne?
                            No

No whippe.

No further runne, then you may turne gaine,
And let not will be guider of your wit.
What needes a plaifter, where there is no paine?
Phyſicke is onely for the crazed fit :
Who is in health, hath not to doe with it.
    Take heede of lying lippes, a ſwearing tongue.
    For they are odious both in old and young.

Haſt thou a wit and knoweſt thou canſt do wel,
Vſe it vnto ſome worke of worth in deede.
For tis no wit, to teach a foole to ſpell
Nothing but foole; when he is learn'd to reed.
Better, to teach him Chriſts croſſe be his ſpeed,
    And how the holy Ghoſt may better guide him,
    Then with conceites of ieſts for to deride him.
                                                    It

No whippe.

It is a courſe of little charitie,
To find out faults,and fall vpon them ſo;
And tis a wit of ſingularitie,
That perfect wiſedom doth but little ſhow:
Which thinks it giues the foole the ouer-throw,
   And might haue bene farre better exerciſed,
   Then in the folly that it hath ſuprized.

Tis womens ieſt to wrangle for a word,
And what thinke women then of wrangling men
Let ſuch fond quarrels be put vnder boord,
As doe but ſpring out of an idle penne.
Oh, trouble not the fowle within the fenne.
   The fame of learning neuer was worſe grac't,
   Then where one foole an other hath defac't.
                                But

No whippe.

But, art thou learned? looke into thy booke,
And thou shalt find thy fancy is abus'd,
Which hath thy hope of happy prayse mistooke;
And done a fault that cannot be excus'd :
For Wisedome neuer such an humour vs'd.
    To shoote at shame, the aime was to farre off,
    To beat downe sinne, to ierke it with a scoffe.

Hawkes hoods, & bels are not for Scholers study,
They haue no argument for wo, ho, ho :
Their spirits should not think on things so muddy,
Where Duckes lie dibbling in the lakes below :
But on the grounds, where sweeter graces grow.
    And though a fault be scused with a iest :
    A iest is but a folly at the best.
                        Let

No whippe.

Let all good Scbollers winde their wits away,
From fuch ill following of their idle wils;
Leaft when they fee their faults another day,
They doe repent them of their little skils,
Where lacke of Grace, a wittie fpirit fpils.
    For drinke is poifon that is drunke in quaffing;
    And wit but folly, that fets fooles a laughing.

Beleeue me, tis a kind of fport to fome
That loue no wit; becaufe of ignorance:
When warres begin, to ftrike a wodden drum.
When vertuous fpirits fall at variance :
About the treading of a Moris-dance.
    But what more fpight can be to a good wit,
    Then fee a foole to ftand and laugh at it?
                         But

No whippe.

But, who will laugh ſo quickly as the foole?
Although he know not well at what indeede:
But who hath liu'd in any learned Schoole,
Would leaue a line for any aſſe to reede;
Except(alas)he were conſtrain'd for neede,
As many are,God knowes(the more the pitty)
That were they wealthy, would be far more witty.

Sigh then for ſuch,to ſee their ſory caſes,
That muſt ſuch treaſure for ſuch traſh, go ſell:
And doe not fall to grieue them with diſgraces,
That in their ſowles doe ſo with ſorrow dwell,
As in their hearts is more than halfe a hell,
   To beat theit braines but for a little gaines,
   And,or be curſt, or ſcoft at for their paines.

                         But

No whippe.

But if there be some nimble wittted Sir,
That loues to play with euery one he sees:
And hath a sport to make a stinking stir
With buzzing verses, like to Humble Bees:
I wish such pride were plucked on his knees,
　　To make him know twere better to be quiet,
　　Then with his wits to runne so farre at riot.

But for my selfe, I know not any such:
Because, perhaps, I haue not read their writings:
Or els, I doubt they are too deepe a tuch,
For the short reach of my poore thoughts inditings,
That could not roue at their conceipts delightings.
　　How ere it be, I know I doe not know them;
　　And therefore care not who do ouerthrow them.
　　　　　　　　　　　　　　　　　　　But

No whippe.

But for my felfe, what euer I haue writ;
And for poore Mad-cap, I dare fweare as much:
In all the compaffe of a little wit,
It meant no one particular to touch.
But for one fhould not at another grutch;
    As the clouds thickend, and the raine did fall,
    He caſt his Cap, at finne in generall.

Indeed, tis true, he caſt his Cap at finne;
And would to God that all the world did fo:
Then doe I hope our fpirits fhould begin,
Our wit, and fenfes better to beſtow,
Then one to feeke anothers ouer-throw.
    But pardon him for what is paſt before,
    And he hath done for capping any more.

                                And

No whippe.

And for my felfe, good brother, by your leaue,
I will not now difpute an Argument
Of what I would, nor what I could conceiue,
Nor what may be difcretions detriment,
In fhewing of a wittie excrement:
    But I will wifh all Scholers fhould be friends,
    And Poets not to brawle for puddings ends.

I am not worthy to be heard to fpeake
Emong the wife, what they fhould haue to doe:
But if there liue a wit that be too weake,
Aduifed care to bring his will vnto:
Oh, with good words let me his fpirit wooe,
    That he will now but onely ftudie *pro*,
    Let *nos* be *nobis*, and the *contra* goe.
               C   So

No whippe.

So shall our Muses sweetest musique make,
When gratious spirits doe agree in one :
And euery foole may not example take
At our vnnaturall dissention :
Let euery Asse goe by himselfe alone :
　And let vs seeme as though we knewe them not,
　Since no more good is by them to be got.

Tell not a Souldier of his bloodie sword,
Nor yet the Sailer of his life at sea :
Nor tell the Courtier of his knife aboord,
Nor tel the Lawier of his gaineful plea :
Nor tell the louer of his little flea :
　Let them alone, and trouble none of them :
　A secret hum is better then a hem.

If

No whippe.

If you will needes be merry with your wits,
Take heede of names, and figuring of natures:
And tell how neere the goofe the gander fits:
Of *Hob* and *Sib*, and of fuch filly creatures:
Of *Croydon* fanguine and of home made features:
 But fkorne them not, for they are honeft people,
 Although perhaps theyneuer faw Paules fteeple.

But, if you could, you fhould doe better much,
To bend your ftudie to a better end,
And neither one nor other feeme to tuch:
But in fuch forte, as may befeeme a friend:
And doe no more your fpirits idly fpend
 With ierking, biting, skoffing and fuch humors
 As fill the world too full of wicked rumors.
C 2   Bring

No whippe.

Bring in no Verſes for Authorities:
As in preſenti, and leaue out the *R:*
Tis fit for Babes in their minorities,
Emong their formes, to fall at ſuch a iarre.
Necke verſes are for theeues but at the Barre.
   God bleſſe vs man from euer comming there:
   A gulitie heart can ſcarcely reade for feare.

Bacchus and *Ceres* were the Gods below:
And there ſhall be, and neuer come aboue.
And Claret wine will quicken wit I trowe:
By the Redde Croſſe, I ſweare, it is to proue:
But, what ſhould Scholers, wine and ſugar moue,
   To bring in ſo *Appollo* and *virorum?*
   When wiſe men ſmile at *horum harum horum.*
                           But,

No whippe.

But, pardon me, if that I speake falfe Latine
For lacke of learning: I no fcholer am:
My mafters gowne deferues no face of Satine:
I neuer to degree of Mafter came:
But, where fmall learning might attaine the fame:
   And for a verfe in Latine, let me fee:
   Alas, they haue too many feete for mee.

But, let me loue that language yet of olde,
For *Ergos* fake, that many a time deluded
My troobled harte, that knewe not what to holde
Should be vpon the confequence concluded,
While many a *Placet* for his place entruded:
   Vntill the Bell bad breake vp fchoole, and then
   Sufficient, made, a world of propre men.

No whippe.

And I among them, not the leaſt contented
To ſee both Maior, and the Minor ceaſe,
Full many a time my haſtie will repented,
When I haue wiſht a Placet hold his peace:
Whoſe Sophyſtrie would ſo my feare increaſe,
　　That to be ſhort, my learning was ſo little,
　　As I may write my Title in a tittle.

Looke not therefore for arguments of Arte:
But from the painted cloth vpon the wall,
What I haue learn'd I kindely doe imparte,
Hoping to purchaſe no ill will at all:
Becauſe, ſo rudely to my worke I fall.
　　Such weakeneſſe my poore wits are come vnto,
　　That beaſts, & birds, muſt teach me what to do.
　　　　　　　　　　　　　　　　　　　My

No whippe.

My Librarie is but experience:
The Authors, Men,that in my notes I finde:
My notes,the natures of such difference,
As may defcry each other in their kinde:
Where,if my wit and fenfes be not blinde,
  I doe perceiue in too much ill defarte:
    Pride in a Scholer, makes a foole by Arte.

Blame me not then, if that I iudge amiffe:
The Sunne and Moone are my Aftronomie:
When you beholde where all my cunning is,
Charge not fimplicitie with villany:
It were enough to breede an Agony
  In many a man: but truely not in me,
    That make no care,what ere your cenfure be.

No whippe.

If it be good, I thanke you for good will:
If contrarie, so contrarie come to you.
If it be well, I can not take it ill:
If otherwise, the like good may it doe you.
If kindely then, as kindly let me wooe you
    To leaue such ierkings, least they smart too sore.
    Loue me as I doe you, I aske no more.

But yet, me thinkes, I see you smile at mee, (ding:
As though my Rules were scarcely worth the rea-
And that a silly painted cloath should be
The Librarie of all my learnings breeding:
And that my wits had need of too much weeding.
    Oh what a burthen must my patience cary?
    The Alehouse is the Asses Dictionary.

                                              But

No whippe.

But for the Alehouſe and the Painted Cloth,
If ought I finde there, that be worth the noting :
Laying aſide the filthy dronken froth :
What good I ſee, I will not skippe the coating.
A good Redde Herring may be worth the bloting.
 Better a good wit in an Alehouſe ſit,
 Then finde an Alehouſe in an idle wit.

So much in honour of my homely booke :
Wherein the Birds and beaſts ſo wiſely ſpeake :
And ſo much for the notes from them I tooke,
To helpe ſuch wits as will hath made too weake,
Into the bounds of bleſſed thoughts to breake.
 Now, for the natures of thoſe notes, you ſee
 What cauſe you haue to thinke amiſſe of me.

I

No whippe.

I will not meddle with *Quæ Maribus*,
The *Propria* will trouble me too much:
Nor yet, *Qui mihi Discipulus:*
Except I knew my mastership were such,
As somewhat might a gratious Scholer tuch.
   No, I will let the Latine lines alone;
   And speake a few more English, and be gone.

Let all good wits, if any good there be;
Leaue trussing, and vntrussing of their points,
And heare thus much (although not learne) of me;
The spirits, that the Oyle of Grace annoyntes,
Will keepe their senses in those sacred ioynts,
   That each true-learned, Christian-harted bro-
   Will be vnwilling to offend another.   (ther
                                And

No whippe.

And ſo would I; for if in truthe, I knewe
(Although it were full much againſt my will)
I ſhould offend but any one of you,
That might conceiue iuſt cauſe to wiſh me ill:
I would throwe downe my Inke,& break my quill,
 Ere I would write one word to ſuch an ende,
 As might but gaine a foe,or loſe a friende.

In kindeneſſe then let me entreate you this:
If that your leaſure ſerue you,looke it ouer:
And what you finde that you may take amiſſe,
Let my confeſſion of ſmall learning couer,
Let euery Poet be each others louer.
 Let vs note follies, and be warned by them :
 But not in writing,to the world deſcry them.

It

No whippe.

It is a plot among pernicious braines,
To breede a brawle twixt better natur'd wits,
By foothing finne with humour of difdaines,
Vntill they fall into fome raging fits,
Wherein the fruite but of Repentance fits:
  But let them liften to thofe tongues that lift,
  Let vs not labour for a Had I wift.

For, fome will fay that Arte is ill beftow'd
On him that knowes not how to vfe it well.
And he fometime may finde his wits befhrow'd,
That reades his leffon ere he learne to fpell:
Marke but the truthe, the painted cloath doth tell;
  Who laies to much vpon his wits at once,
  May happe to prooue an Ideot for the nonce.
                                        Sound

No whippe.

Sound a mans minde before you ſhew his meaning:
For feare repentance come an houre too late.
Barre nor the beggers from their merry gleaning:
Except the Land-lord bid you keepe the gate:
And where you may haue loue, hunt not for hate.
   Let Poets drinke of *Helicons* faire fountaine,
    But bring no Mice out of a ſwelling mountaine.

Let Noddies go to cuffes for bloudie noſes:
Let vs but laugh to ſee their lack of reaſon:
Leaue them their weedes, and let vs gather Roſes,
And reap our wheat, while they do pick on peaſon.
Let vs hate lies, ingratitude, and treaſon,
   And with our friends in fond conceipts to ſtriue,
   And we ſhall be the bleſſed'ſt men aliue.
If

No whippe.

If that a minde be full of misery,
VVhat villany is it to vexe it more?
And if a wench doe treade her shooe awry,
VVhat honest heart will turne her out of dore?
Oh, if our faultes were all vpon the skore:
    VVhat man so holy, but would be ashamed,
      To heare himselfe vpon the Schedule named?

Let vs then leaue our biting kinde of verses:
They are too bitter for a gentle taste.
Sharpe pointed speach so neare the spirit pearces,
As growes to rankle ere the poison waste.
But let all be forgotten that is past:
    And let vs all agree in one in this;
      Let God alone to mend what is amisse.

                                       But

No whippe.

But if we needes will try our wits to write,
And ftriue to mount our Mufes to the height,
Oh let vs labour for that heauenly light,
That may direct vs in our paffage ftreight:
V Vhere humble wits may holy will awaite;
   And there to finde that worke to write & reede,
   That may be worth the looking on indeede.

To fhewe the life of vnitie in loue,
V Vhere neuer difcord doth the mufique marre:
But, in the bleffing of the foules behoue,
To fee the light of that faire fhining ftarre,
V Vhich fhews the day that neuer night can marre:
   But in the brightneffe of eternall glory,
   How loue and life doe make a bleffed ftory.

                                    If

No whippe.

If we be toucht with sorrow of our sinnes,
Expresse our passions as the Psalmist did:
And shew how mercy, hopes reliefe beginnes,
Where geatest harmes are in repentance hid:
When Grace in Mercy doth despaire forbid:
   And sing of him, and of his glory such,
   Who hateth sinne, yet will forgiue so much.

And let our hymnes be Angell harmonie,
Where *Halleluiah* makes the heauens to ring:
And make a consort of such companie,
As make the Quire but to their holy King:
This, this, I say, would be a blessed thing:
   When all the world might ioy to heare and see
   How Poets, in such Poetry agree.

For

No whippe.

For who can make an Ape to leaue his mowes,
Although he call him twentie times an Ape?
And who can ſtop the cawing of the Crowes,
Although he tell them of their carrion gape?
And if the collicke chance to breed a ſcape,
　But hold your noſe the ſent will quickly die:
　Then cry not foh; but let the fih goe by.

A Maſtiffe dog will neuer make a Spaniell:
Then let the Curre alone to ſhew his kinde.
A horſe-mans ſaddle is no market paniell.
To waſh a Moore is worke againſt the winde.
Thoſe blinking wits do ſhow their wils too blind,
That finding faultes ſo roughly fall vpon them,
To think to mend them with their railing on them

No whippe.

The deuill is a knaue, who knowes it not?
And who but God, can put downe all his power?
And how muſt God his gracious loue be got?
But all by prayer euery day and houre;
While teares of ſorrow make a bleſſed ſhowre:
　And humble faith doth but to mercy flie,
　In hearty prayer; not in Poetry.

Yet ſay I not, but Poets well may pray;
And praying Poets doe moſt ſweetly ſing.
For proofe, of *Dauid* ſee what trueth may ſay;
A praying Poet, and a bleſſed King:
Whoſe verſes all did from ſuch vertues ſpring,
　As left the loue of learned trueth to try,
　Howe prayer ſhewes the princely Poetry.

Let

No whippe.

Let vs all Poets then agree together,
To run from hell, and fained *Helicon*;
And looke at heauen, and humbly hie vs thither,
Where Graces ſhall be let in,euery one,
To ſing a part in Glories vnion;
    And there to ſettle all our ſoules deſire,
    To heare the muſicke of that heauenly Quire.

Let *Ouid*,with *Narciſſus* idle tale,
Weare out his wits with figuratiue fables.
Old idle Hiſtories grow to be ſo ſtale,   (tables,
That clownes almoſt haue bard them from their
And *Phœbus*, with his horſes,and his ſtables:
    Leaue them to babies:make a better choiſe
    Of ſweeter matter for the ſoules reioyce.
D 2   Who

No whippe.

Who toucheth pitch and tarre cannot be cleane.
A wilfull wit doth worke it felfe much woe.
In euery courfe tis good to keepe a meane:
And being well, to liue contented fo.
The foftest walkers doe moft fafely goe.
  Haft maketh waft:and wits that run aftray,
  Make had I wift,to make fooles holy-day.

Be quiet then,I fay;be quiet, Wagges:
And haue no more with nothing worth to doe:
While other angle for the golden bagges,
We feeke out toies,to fet our wits vnto:
But let vs leaue the Cobbler to his fhooe.
  And let the foole, himfelfe with folly flatter:
  And bend our ftudies vnto better matter.

No

No whippe.

No: this is not a world for simple wits,
That can not looke a mile aboue the Moone:
Nor roste their sparrowes but on wodden spits:
Nor make a morning of an after-noone:
Nor watch a blessing when there fals a Boone:
  No, no: it is no world for weake conceit.
  The Deuil is too cunning in deceit.

A silly honest creature may do well,
To watch a cockeshoote or a limed bush:
For many a Scholler happly learnes to spell,
That can not put together worth a rush;
Yet let a Poet at such humors hush:
  His will should be about some other worke,
  Then where the Adder in the grasse doth lurke.
                    D 3   And

No whippe.

And since my selfe haue marched in that ranke,
VVhere *Mercury* commanded *Pallas* Traine,
And spent my spirits in my thoughts, as franke
As he that thought he had a better vaine:
I must confesse, what idle humours gaine;
    A frumpe, a frowne, a foyle, or els a feare:
    VVhen wil doth write that reason cannot beare.

No, truely no : this world is not for me.
I will no longer be fantasticall;
But winke at folly, when the foole I see:
That in his gesture is so finicall,
As if his spirit were Poeticall :
    And thinke it better weare my wits at Schoole,
    Then spoyle my wits in painting of a foole.
                       Vpon

No whippe.

Vpon the painted cloth, the Nightingale
Did bid me heare,and fee,and fay the beft.
The fea Mew fayes it is a cruel gale,
That driues the Swallow cleane out of her neft.
Why,fimple nofes now can bide no ieft:
    And Poets,that are open in Inuectiues,
    Doe often fall vpon too much defectiues.

Beleeue me brother,tis as thou doeft write;
Poets fhould wright by heauenly infpiration:
But he that is poffeffed with defpight,
Shewes but a wicked kinde ofinftigation;
To thinke by fcoffes to make a reformation.
    No,let vs all goe backe to vertues Schooles,
    And let the world alone to bring vp fooles.

No whippe.

I haue bene vaine as any man aliue:
But would be vertuous now, if I knew how:
And euery day, and houre, and minute ſtriue
My wicked heart to better grace to bow.
Then let me ſay, as to my ſelfe, to you;
   Let vs leaue all our idle imperfeƈtions,
   And ſtudy vertue, for our liues direƈtions:

Let vs ſerue God, in word, and deed, and thought;
And by our ſilence make our quarrels ceaſe:
And learne thoſe leſſons that true loue hath taught,
Where concord doth a bleſſed world encreaſe,
And ſpeake of Peace, or let vs hold our peace.
   For words, or deeds, or thoughts of ſtrife are e-
   And are but inſtigations of the Deuill.   (uill,
                                    It

No whippe.

It is a fhame to fhun the way of Grace,
And run our wits a gathering after wool;
And finde the haire fo courfe in euery place,
As makes a wood-cocke proue himfelfe a Gull,
That hath no better braines within his fcull,
   Then to beftow his time in idle trifles,
    With penning notes to fil the world with nifles.

For God fake let vs then our follies leaue,
And not lay open one anothers ill;
But in our confcience learne for to conceiue,
How heedleffe wit may be abuf'd by will,
And haue a care fo well to vfe our skill,
   We may be loued for our learned lines,
    Where gracious fpirits Poets make Diuines.
                        And

No whippe.

And for my felfe, I meane the Ice to breake,
Vnto the paffage of that Paradice;
VVhere rauifht Grace may of that Glory fpeake,
VVhere mercy liues,and comfort neuer dyes,
And the beft praife of any Poet lies :
   Or at the leaft if any went before,
   Follow that line,and loue the world no more.

What right bred wits, will haue to doe with blind
Efpecially blind beggers and their boyes? (men,
They that haue iudgement,how indeed to find men
VVil think fuch younkers but hobberdie-hoyes,
That ply their wits vnto fuch paltrie toyes :
   Or els to fhew that he hath learn'd in part,
   To rob the blindeman of his beggers art.

If

No whippe.

If it be ſo, and meane to keepe a Schoole
To bring vp boyes vnto the beggers crafte,
To take a threſholde, for his cuſhen-ſtoole,
To knaue a cruſt, and drinke a ſorry draft,
Let him goe ſleepe when he hath ſoundly quaft,
    And ſhrugge himſelfe vnder ſome ſorry tree,
ˋ. And, 'mong the beggers, maſter begger be.

But then me thinkes he ſhould ſet out his table;
All ye that ſeeke to haue your children taught,
To play the begger how he may be able,
VVhen that his eye-ſight groweth old, or naught:
Aske for the man that hath the Cony caught,
And dwelleth, where the matter is not great:
And you ſhall haue them boorded without meate.
                                      But

No whippe.

But tis no matter: men that haue a name,
Neede make no table; they are knowen so well.
And the blinde Begger hath so great a fame,
As of his trickes can euery high-way tell.
And since for begging he doth beare the bell,
    Let him keepe Schoole; and learne of him that
    The stocks wil kindly fit him for his skill. (will:

But for I doubt, some men of good profession,
Will take exceptions at my table-writing:
To honest mindes I make my hearts confession;
My soule is free from vertuous spirits spighting:
Not one of them is in my thoughts endighting.
    I rather wish, God blesse them and their Arts,
    And let the blind men play the Beggers parts.
                                        For

No whippe

For all good Poets will cry out vpon him,
That falles to blindenes and to beggery:
And in his wits, be fo farre woe-begon him,
That in an humour, of bafe trumpery,
The world may fee, in idle foolery,
   A Ballad-maker would haue bene a Poet:
   But hat he knew not in what point to fhew it.

Thus will the world be defcanting on writers,
When they fhall read their ouer-rude defcriptions,
And fay that fpirits which are growen fuch fpigh-
Shuld better learned be in loues prefcriptions; (ters
Then goe about fo with their circumfcriptions:
   That wits of worth, that know their foolery,
   Doe call it Pot-rie, and not Poetrie.

And

No whippe.

And what haue we to doe with pilgrimage,
To walke bare witted to S. Dunces well?
A Grammer Scholer but of ten yeeres age,
That fcarfe hath learn'd his Latine lines to fpell,
VVill foone by heart, a better ftory tell:
    And fay, fuch Poets as their wits fo toffe,
    Make all their walkes by little witttam croffe.

For let the world imagine what it lift,
And idle wits deceiue themfelues with toyes :
Thofe hammeringheads that breedbut HadI wift,
Are all to farre from thofe affured ioyes,
VVhere heauenly comfort kils al earths annoyes.
    No,no: tis onely Vnitie and Peace,
    That makes all bleffings profper and encreafe.
                      Oh,

No whippe

Oh Poets, turne the humour of your braines,
Vnto ſome heauenly Muſe, or meditation;
And let your ſpirits there imploy your paines,
VVhere neuer weary, needs no recreation,
VVhile God doth bleſſe each gracious cogitation.
   For proud compariſons are alwayes odious:
   But humble Muſes muſicke is melodious.

Then learne to ſing, and leaue to learne to braule.
It is vnfitting to a fine conceit,
   From vertues care, to vaine effects to fall,
   VVhere careleſſe words doe carry little weight,
   VVhile fancie angles but with follies baite:
   VVhich, hanging but a Gudgin on the hooke,
   May ſigh to ſee, what idle paines he tooke.
                            No,

No whippe.

No,no: let fancie weane her ſelfe from folly;
And heauenly prayers grace our Poetrie.
Let vs not loue the thought that is not holy,
Nor bend our mindes to blinde mens beggerie:
But let vs thinke it our ſoules miſery,
   That all our Muſes doe not ioyne in one,
   To make a Quire to ſing to God alone.

Eor could our ſpirits all agree together,
In the true ground of vertues humble grace,
To ſing of heauen,and of the high-way thither,
And of the ioyes in that moſt ioyfull place,   .
Where Angels armes the bleſſed ſoules embrace;
Then God himſelfe would bleſſe our ſoules endi-
And al the world would loue a Poets writing.(ting,
     FINIS.